Critical

"The language is simple and the descriptions are precise. Espinal is able to put together a complex puzzle from a few pieces. ...When Espinal decides to enter the narrative and give herself the license to interpret, she does so with a sharpness that proves how promising her voice is. For example, "Singing is an act that belongs to the past. Talk too. What I say is in the past, I do not even remember it. My words are forgotten, my thoughts, my songs. What I sang yesterday does not exist any-more. The difference is in the public, in the witnesses, they are the ones that make for- getting difficult. If there is someone who hears what you have to say, he/she may remember it; if there are two, it is more likely. And there is the explanation: they seek fame because they fear oblivion. I do not!"

- El Espectador

"This story is a blow to adolescent dreams, those dreams we all have that don't change too much as the years go by, dreams that turn into frustration, fixed in certain moments like the flags of worlds we'll never conquer. But in a world that urges us con-stantly to seek attention from others, Espinal Solano suggests that perhaps our gifts and talents are their own reward."

- Revista Arcadia

Another critic asserts *"... What connected me to the novel is the honesty in the introspective narration of self-discovery... the lyricism that this work possesses caught me without my being able to do anything about it."*

I'd like you to hear the song
I'm listening to as I write this

I'd like you to hear the song
I'm listening to as I write this

By

Manuela Espinal Solano

Translated by Jeannine Pitas

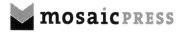

Library and Archives Canada Cataloguing in Publication

Title: I wish you could hear the song I'm listening to as I write this...
/ Manuela Espinal Solano.

Other titles: Quisiera que oyeran la canción que escucho cuando
escribo esto. English | I wish you could hear the song I
am listening to as I write this...

Names: Espinal Solano, Manuela, 1998- author. | Pitas, Jeannine
Marie, translator.

Description: Translation of: Quisiera que oyeran la canción que
escucho cuando escribo esto.

Translated by Jeannine Pitas.

Identifiers: Canadiana (print) 20210255234
Canadiana (ebook) 20210256885

ISBN 9781771615242 (softcover) ISBN 9781771615259 (PDF)
ISBN 9781771615266 (EPUB) ISBN 9781771615273 (Kindle)

Classific ation: LCC PQ8180.415.S65 Q5713 2021
DDC 863/.7—dc23

Published by Mosaic Press, Oakville, Ontario, Canada, 2022.

MOSAIC PRESS, Publishers
www.Mosaic-Press.com

English Copyright © Mosaic Press 2022, Translated by Jeannine Pitas.

Originally Published in Spanish Quisiera que oyeran la canción que
escucho cuando escribo esto © Editorial Angosta, 2016

Cover Photo by Pablo Monsalve

Printed and bound in Canada

ONTARIO ARTS COUNCIL
CONSEIL DES ARTS DE L'ONTARIO
an Ontario government agency
un organisme du gouvernement de l'Ontario

Funded by the Government of Canada
Financé par le gouvernement du Canada

Canadä

ONTARIO
CREATES

MOSAIC PRESS
1252 Speers Road, Units 1 & 2, Oakville, Ontario, L6L 5N9
(905) 825-2130 • info@mosaic-press.com • www.mosaic-press.com

The Novella that has become a sensation in Colombia, written by an eighteen year old! Published in Colombia, Spain, Peru, Ecuador and Bolivia

Born in Medellin in 1998, Espinal Solano wrote this novella for a youth literary contest while she was in high school in 2016. She did not win the competition, but her work was discovered and quickly published by Editorial Angosta. Written in the first person, the semi-autobiographical coming-of-age story introduces us to a young woman who has grown up in a musical family. Her mother and grandmother are professional singers. There is not one family member who is not an amateur, semi-professional or professional vocalist, instrumentalist or both. The original title of the novella was Herencia -Inheritance – and it raises a question that is shared by all of us – which aspects of our upbringing and family background should we choose to preserve or is imposed on us for the duration of adult lives? What do we inherit willingly or unwillingly, what do we reject, what do we rebel against, what scares remain, what do we recreate?

This novella explores the classic tale of adolescent rebellion but it is more complex. How do young people deal with the apparent univer- sal desire for attention and fame? The social media today have made the fulfillment of this desire accessible to more people. But this work explores this issue very personally and deeply. When the young nar- rator asks her grandmother why is everyone in their family so eager to perform as a musician, the grandmother challenges her by stating "Who in this world doesn't want to be famous? Who would shy away from attention, notoriety? Who would want to hide their talent?"

Translator support

Mosaic Press acknowledges the support from Reading Colombia which contributed to the publication of this English language edition.

A selection
of contemporary
Colombian authors

For Mom and J.
the protagonists of many other stories
For D.

I'd like you to hear the song
I'm listening to as I write this

I remember the day we went to Bogotá. We were looking for something different, a new opportunity for all three of us. We brought everything we had, and we didn't look back. The idea was to live there for a short time while waiting for our visas to be processed, and once we got them we'd set off again, for a place even farther away. Canada – that was the country my mother hoped to reach. So we, like loyal little chicks obeying their mother hen, followed her to the taxi stand, to the airport, to Bogotá. We followed her even when we had to go back to Medellín because the plan didn't work out, at least not in the way Mom had hoped.

We landed in Bogotá because Mom got a gig as a singer in a restaurant.

During the time before that journey, Mom sang in bars, in restaurants, at parties. She always left the house wearing a shining, elegant dress, her big eyes made up to look like those of a cat; her cheeks were always dusted in rouge; her lips were red, her body tanned. Later she'd return home tired, with less makeup on her face, holding her shoes in her hand. My sister and I were already all too familiar with this routine.

On one of those work days, all dressed and ready, Mom left the house, kissed us goodbye and got into a cab. We waved at her from the window.

"I need to get to the Piano Bar," she told the driver.

The Piano Bar was a popular nightlife spot where people would go to eat, drink, and hang out. Young adults loved it but kids weren't allowed inside, so we waited at home, imagining the dances, the food, the conversations. Mom always talked about how great it was working there – the smell, the people, the music. I wanted to see it. Only once did I get close: one night, for no apparent reason, my family decided to go to the restaurant next door for dinner. They'd reserved a table for twenty, as if we were a large family. I played it cool; I got up and secretly asked my grandmother if I could go and use the washroom. She nodded. I walked slowly, stepping down the hallway where the washrooms were, the hallway that led directly to a parking lot shared by the two restaurants. I stepped outside, weaving around cars and bumping into a few side mirrors until I got as close to the Piano Bar as I needed to be: I could see how the lights were shining through the windows.

I could hear the sounds coming from inside; the young people were stepping out to smoke, the older ones to talk. The music sounded like rock, and the laughter and conversations were easily heard. A smell of grilled meat hung in the air. I could see the grill; I could hear the barbecue sizzling; I got so close to the people that I could sense the saliva of one customer who was dying to taste that meat. I could hear the fizzle of bubbles in the soft drinks sipped by those who opted to avoid alcohol. Right there, so close to the Piano Bar, without even going in. But Mom wasn't singing there that night.

That happened on a different night. Mom arrived at the Piano Bar at nine. The owner of the establishment came up to her. "Hi! You got here just in time," he said in a kind way and with a big smile.

Mom smiled and replied, "I'll start whenever you tell me."

"Listen, tonight we have some VIPs coming, so it would be good if you could sing some more subtle pieces – Let's have calm, gentle songs tonight."

The show began with "Sabor Sabor" by Rosario Flores. I'd already heard Mom sing this song. She practised her repertoire almost daily on the green floral couch whose various colours could be found throughout the rest of the house. She sat right there, in the middle of the room, and repeated the songs again and again. I knew almost all the lyrics. I loved watching Mom there, singing so peacefully, just her and her voice without any audience.

Mom moved slowly on stage, relishing each song. Her dress moved with her, the sequins reflecting the lights of the room, her shoes tapping on the floor, an accompaniment to the melody. People made their comments on seeing her: "She looks good...She's a pretty girl...She's very talented...My daughter's already five... Today I went to the doctor and..." Mom smiled and strolled about the stage as the owner had requested. That night she sang a varied repertoire, following instructions she'd been given. She came down from the stage at nearly one in the morning. The waiter offered her a drink and, as always, she requested a glass of lemonade. She drank it slowly, her gaze fixed to the floor, tapping her feet to the rhythm of a Maná song playing in the background. She was tired. But then, someone came up to her.

"Hello," said Mom, curious.

"Hello. I was watching you up there, your dancing, singing. You really shine," the stranger said.

"Wow, thanks so much," said Mom, laughing nervously.

"I have a restaurant in Bogotá. I don't know what you'll think of this, but I'd love it if you could be my regular singer there."

For a minute or more Mom said nothing. She knew that this could be the perfect opportunity to get her visa processed – something she'd been wanting to do for a long time.

The man informed Mom that he was going to stay a few more days in Medellín, so she could take some time to give it more thought.

*

The days got longer. One week passed, then two. He stayed a month, two months in Medellín, as if he weren't needed back at his own restaurant. But this time together allowed him and Mom to get to know each other, to go out and talk about her plan to live and work in Bogotá. The man sold Mom on the idea that a new life in the capital would be the best possible investment for her and for us. My sister and I hadn't met him yet, but Mom talked a lot about him, the plan, the job, the new life we'd have. Not only did he convince her to travel; they also developed a strong friendship.

In the end he went back to Bogotá happy to have hired the singer he enjoyed so much that night at the Piano Bar.

The contract that Mom signed meant that she would be the singer there for three months. She had requested this for several reasons: she was excited to travel, but she was apprehensive and didn't want to commit for a longer period. Also, three months was the amount of time that would be needed for us to get our visas. The contract included an apartment for the three of us to live in. One month later we packed our bags and set off.

*

It was the year 2010. I don't remember what month it was, so there's no point in trying to mention what day. We reached Bogotá. I was thirteen years old. Bogotá is quite chilly compared to Medellín. It has terrible traffic jams and is consumed by buildings, but I was excited to go there.

After just a few days we already knew the way to reach the restaurant on foot. You just had to leave the house, turn left and walk three blocks before hitting the main road; from there, the path was straight. You had to walk straight for four blocks, then cross the fourth street and turn left; there you'd find the *zona rosa* – the busy nightlife and entertainment district. One, two, three – the fourth establishment was the restaurant where Mom worked.

The way to the restaurant and the way to the theatre school were the only directions I knew. I had to learn them; they were the places I visited most often. The only things on my agenda were visiting my Mom at the restaurant, going to theatre class, eating in the restaurant, going to theatre class, returning to the restaurant to pick up the house keys, going to theatre class. This is how my days were spent. I liked that routine.

Mom had little time for a social life or leisure activities. She went back and forth between work and getting our visas processed. For the time being, everything was going fine. She received some of the necessary paperwork that our grandparents had sent from Medellín; she filled out forms, made phone calls. I observed this and assumed that everything was under control. She was busy, but my sister and I didn't have too much to do. While living in Bogotá we did not go to school; therefore, we had plenty of free time and asked Mom if she could please find something for us to do while waiting for everything to fall into place so that we could study, live and work in the country that she had chosen. That's how she ended up looking for theatre schools for us.

Our classes began after we'd been in Bogotá for two weeks. We checked out several schools; we spent one whole day looking at posters, inquiring about prices. We'd leave one school and immediately go to another. We visited a lot of them. Some were quite big and recommended by everyone, with large spaces and professional lighting. Others were smaller and known to just a few, with natural light only – their classes finished as soon as it got dark.

We chose DECA, a school at the north end of the city. DECA was actually an old house that a group of theatre professionals took over after negotiating with the State to make it their headquarters. We were drawn to the leaves of a climbing plant that scaled the windows of that house. The whole facade was decorated. Inside we found a surprise; the place was full; there were students, parents, people who had come just to see the place, and a national theatre group that was rehearsing for a play they were putting on a few weeks later. There was plenty of activity, and that drew our interest.

It was a big place. The first floor had three large class-rooms and a theatre for shows. There were two more floors above it. The second level had four rooms with wooden floors that were noisy when you tapped your feet on them. The third floor was one large room. It was the most important part of the building because it was the rehearsal space for the actors who put on the musical the-atre production, which was the biggest event the school organized. We met Daniel Calderón, the school's owner and the source of its name, DECA. Mom introduced her-self as a singer from Medellín. Daniel smiled in wonder:

"What about these kids?" he asked.

"My daughters. They also sing. They're the best I've heard."

Daniel smiled again. The conversation lasted a while, until he said he had to go – he had a whole room full of people waiting for his class. We decided that my sister and I would take an intermediate acting class, with children our age, because we already had some experience – we'd taken an acting class in Medellín – and he warned us that the classes had begun one month prior and that they were already in the final stages of putting on a production.

"And have you thought about signing up for classes yourself?" Daniel asked Mom.

"No. I don't act."

"I think you have potential. Also, you're a singer, which is exactly what we need. We're doing a musical."

He didn't have to twist her arm. It was decided. The following week we started our acting classes. My sister and I in an intermediate-level course, full of children with whiny voices, children shorter than normal for their age. Mom was placed right into a leading role in the musical.

*

According to the stories, the family legends, and personal testimony I managed to coax out of my grandmother, she was the first in the family to be gainfully employed as a singer. Before her, no one had seen music as a viable career choice. Nevertheless, all the family members that my grandmother could remember had been musicians: amateurs, enthusiasts, instrumentalists who'd play at parties in their homes, playing for themselves, their families, their loved ones, enjoying an anonymity that some well-known musicians would envy. I asked who sang before she did.

"We all sang. We all liked music. In fact, I was the only one who didn't learn to play an instrument," she told me as if she had a debt to music that, despite everything, she'd never managed to repay.

I was struck by the idea that they were all musicians. Yes, we all sang. We were all born singers. My grandmother's mother, my great-grandmother, sang constantly while cooking; my grandmother's father sang and played the guitar for the children in the family; my grandmother's sisters sang and recited poems at church; my grandmother's two brothers sang in bars by night and did penance for their sins on Sunday mornings with gorgeous anthems in the church choir. The tradition was an unbroken chain. After my grandmother's generation came my mother's. My mother, who had always sung, who'd made a living as a singer. My aunt, who has a job as an English teacher but relapses every so often; she goes back to her roots and sings for what few pesos she can get. And then there's my generation, a smaller generation: just my sister, my cousin and me. We're another story.

*

My grandmother has never stopped singing.

"I've always sung. I've always worn shimmering dresses and lots of makeup. That's me," she says, making gestures of pride, of grandiosity.

"And what is it about music? Where does it come from, this love of singing on stage for an audience?" I ask.

"Who in this world doesn't want to be famous?" she responds, surprised. "Who would shy away from attention, notoriety? Who would want to hide their talent? I don't know one such person, sweetie. Not one."

It's true, she doesn't know any such person; she's always been surrounded by people who love all that: music, attention, talent, fame.

"Who would want to hide their talent?" my grandmother asks me.

"I would," I say in a soft voice. Then I leave the kitchen.

*

When you came out of the elevator, the door was on the left. First there was the dining room, which wasn't very large, just one small table with four little chairs, but it looked good in the middle of our home. The living room was toward the left, with two pieces of furniture and a large window that lit the house during the day and let the cold in at night. A little beyond the living room, but still lit by the window, there was a small studio with one piece of furniture and a set of shelves with two or three books someone had forgotten and ten magazines that would assume the role of our best friends in the games where we pretended to be back in our Medellín school with the friends and teachers we'd left behind. At the front of the dining room there was a door that separated it from the kitchen, which was wood finishing in the corners, with a four-way stove and a large, grey refrigerator. There were exactly three plates, the silverware counted out so that each one had a spoon, fork and knife to go with it. In the back there was a patio with a window and an added-on room so small that it looked like a closet. There stood the sink and washing machine. At the back of the apartment was the room that I shared with my sister, right alongside the bathroom. It was not a large room, but it was just right for the two of us. It had a huge closet, a window we always covered with a heavy curtain to keep the sun out, and a television that only showed the state-run channels. Alongside ours was Mom's room, much bigger and brighter than ours. It had a window that let the sun in each day, a large closet with a clothing rack, and a bathroom.

*

Theatre class was the best part of the day. Rehearsal began immediately after the students arrived. There was no time to explain things; everyone knew what to say, how and when to enter and leave the stage. There was never time to teach us something new, like how to cry. I wanted to learn this skill because it seemed necessary for acting; also, whenever I cried I looked terrible, like I was doing it all wrong. My nose turned red even after I shed just one tear; it looked like my cheeks were swelling to a huge size; my eyes also swelled. And whenever I tried to avoid all this humiliation and refused any attempt to cry, I felt a burning in my throat. I was doing it wrong. But they didn't teach us how to cry. Hard-pressed to find a way to fit my sister and me into the production, they gave us both roles. The teacher had to make up two new characters for us, and we only had a few lines.

When I told Mom about the minor roles we'd been given, that we hardly appeared in the show at all, her face changed; she looked sad or angry. She wanted us out in front, singing; she wanted them to bring out a grand piano and have me sit before it, even though I didn't know how to play. I took on her anger and decided it was true, that I deserved that leading role, that I should be the main character. But why wasn't I? "You have the talent to do it," Mom always said.

I almost never played those leading roles. But even now, as I write this, Mom still says I could.

A few days ago we were watching TV. In one of the commercials that's been on lately a young singer appears, someone new to the industry, and they announce that he's the new host of a TV talent show. Only my age, and he's already well known, already hosting a program. I paid it no notice; I've never wanted to be in the spotlight. But Mom disagreed, sitting on the edge of the bed, turned away from me. She leaned forward a little as if she were going to turn and face me, but she didn't do it. Instead, she kept looking at the television. "You're much more talented than him. You and your sister should be doing something like that."

It's hard to understand. What does she mean by "something like that?" She never says exactly what she wants me to do. I've never actually known.

In any case, my role in the show was quite irrelevant and I was happy. I thought that the teacher was looking at me with that smile on her face because she knew I was more talented than all the other girls. She knew I deserved to play the leading role, but how was she going to take the role away from that little girl who came to each rehearsal, always on time, never missing even one? I thought it was enough that she knew I had talent.

We put on the show twice, and the second time, our villain disappeared. When, looking around, no one saw her in the theatre, they easily reached a consensus: I would replace her. I already knew all the lines, and the villain's part was my favourite. Mom sat in the audience and watched me, smiling the entire time.

*

It had been a while since I'd seen Mom that nervous. She'd been coming home from work nearly every day in a bad mood. She'd leave her high-heeled shoes outside our door and I'd have to go and get them. She'd throw herself down on the bed and ask me to close the door. There wasn't much conversation between us during those days. I thought maybe something was wrong with her theatre classes, but that wasn't it.

One afternoon, she went to the supermarket. My sister and I stayed home alone – she was sleeping and I was alert, watching our home, looking after her, as if there were something actually dangerous to worry about. I stayed in our room and waited for Mom to come home. The phone rang, and I walked slowly, lazily, until I reached it.

"Hello?" I answered.

"I need to talk to your mother," he said. It was the owner of the restaurant.

"Oh, um, she's not here," I said, a little nervously.

"Really? She's never home nowadays. I guess she's at one of her little theatre classes," he said, sounding angry.

"Actually not. She's at the grocery store," I said, confused.

"Fine. I'll call back later."

He hung up. He didn't sound good, I thought. As soon as Mom arrived, I told her about the call and how angry the man had seemed.

"Don't ever answer the phone again. You hear me?"

She looked really upset. I considered trying to give her an explanation. I could have said that I only answered the phone expecting a familiar voice, thinking it might in fact be her calling to check in, or my grandparents calling from Medellín, or our acting teacher. But I said nothing.

*

It was taking a while to put the musical together. All
the kids were saying it would be staged abroad. I didn't
believe that, but it was exciting to think that Mom might
go to another country and live for a while as she'd dreamed
of living – only to come back tired and wanting to stay
here in Bogotá, in my country.

After putting on my group's show, my only task was to
watch the rehearsals for the musical. The young people practised on Tuesdays and Thursdays at the academy and sometimes they also met outside of class time to refine the songs,
dances and dialogue. Those rehearsals were almost always
at our house. Watching them was my favourite thing of all.

The show told a story of five women that were in
prison for different crimes. The first, Rosa, had killed

her husband – that was kind of a cliché, but the character was well-developed. Camila had made a million dollars by some illegal means I can't quite recall, but she hadn't killed anyone. Johanna was a young woman; her mother had died nearly two years prior and she'd kept on cashing her cheques with papers that hadn't been updated. Estela, the oldest, had been in prison for twenty years for some unknown reason. Everyone respected and loved her; everyone knew who she was. And then there was Juliana, a young woman who'd ended up in a prostitution ring because she needed money for her studies. But the show's real attraction was the way these different stories were absurdly connected through flashbacks, choreography, kisses and songs.

All the other characters were secondary. The women's husbands entered the show through memories and visits to the prison. There were also the prisoners' children, brought to the prison by their grandmothers, now growing and no longer remembering their own mothers. The cast was so big that there were also extras, people who were only there to stand in the background or pretend they were talking to someone.

The rehearsals were long. In the academy each rehearsal lasted three hours maximum. But they continued with extra practice in our home, going on for five or six hours. Sometimes, the participants who lived farthest away ended up staying over.

Since the cast had seen the show *Onqotô*, by the Brazilian group Corpo, the rehearsals always began with the song "Pesar do mundo." They watched those bodies moving effortlessly, slowly sliding over the floor, lifting and throwing each other, embracing, moving as one like a school of fish. This was the warm-up song for each rehearsal, and eventually Corpo's choreography was adapted as part of the show.

Mom had a leading role as one of the prisoners. I liked the idea that she was doing something outside of work, even though her job was to sing and she was doing the same thing in the show. It was strange to watch them rehearsing something that was more than just music. It was a break in my routine. At home I was used to listening as Mom rehearsed her songs, but she'd never done something like this. I liked watching them fight, getting dirty in imaginary mud.

One day, when everyone had left the house after the rehearsal, Mom went in the bathroom. I needed to tell her something and followed her; I found the door ajar. She was leaning over the sink, staring intently at her reflection in the mirror. Suddenly, she shrugged and let her head fall down between her shoulders. I heard a little laugh that seemed to come from her chest. She lifted her gaze and began a dialogue. She was asking herself questions and answering them, her face all seriousness. I looked on from outside, trying to decipher what she was saying.

"Your visa has been approved," she said at the end, looking at herself once more in that mirror.

She let out a big laugh and lowered her head again. She tried to calm down and began again. She stood up straight, furrowed her brow a little and began again with the questions. Suddenly she saw me, turned around in surprise, smiled, stroked her face and declared, "It can't be that hard."

And then she stepped out of the bathroom.

*

The year is 1960. My grandmother and grandfather have been dating for a year and have come to relate to each other on many levels, but especially through their shared love of music. My grandmother sings; on stage she is loose and free; she is part of Medellín's municipal choir and has recently met my grandfather there; more than anything else she hopes to become famous. My grandfather sings, plays the guitar and is going crazy over my grandmother. He's in the choir because he enjoys the music, but he also really likes seeing that lovely young woman each day at 8 a.m.

Singing in this choir was the best option for someone who aspired to a musical career and was just starting to discover their talent, but my grandparents already had plenty of musical experience. At that point my grandfather had sung the third part in various trios as well as playing guitar; my grandmother had sung in many bars and restaurants. More than anything else, they were in the choir to see each other.

It was 7:30 a.m. And my grandmother, who at that point was not yet my grandmother, was already late for choir rehearsal. She'd woken up not feeling well, and she was getting tired of the choir; she wanted to do her own thing; she wanted her name on a theatre's marquee; she wanted to sing her own songs. She arrived at the theatre where they were practising; she took a seat in the second row of the audience as quietly as she could so the conductor wouldn't see she'd walked in late. The conductor turned toward her in silence, looking her up and down, not removing his gaze for an instant. He stared at her, blinking quickly with no change of expression, serious and calm. He furrowed his brow a little. There she was, calmly seated in the second row, waiting. Her eyes were small, half-open. Honey-coloured eyes. With complete serenity, in a low, determined voice, the conductor said it:

"You're out."

He was so calm that my grandmother didn't realize he was talking to her. She didn't understand that she'd just been kicked out.

"You're out of this choir, I mean. In case you don't understand."

He said nothing more and turned his back to the choir. He turned his back on his most talented student.

There was no time for anything. There was no explanation. "I'm late because..." No. There was no excuse and she had no desire to make one. She left the theatre, and of course my grandfather followed. This was the greatest gift she'd received; the director removed her without making her give any explanation or pretend she didn't want to leave. He kicked her out and she did not protest. She left the theatre, the choir, because that was what she wanted to do.

*

My grandparents founded the Trio Fantasía, their first musical group, with their Ecuadoran friend Elizabeth Villareal. The second voice in the group has changed many times over these fifty-four years and that dear friend of theirs, Elizabeth, was the first of many who'd come to claim the middle spot. One of them was Mom.

Talking about that trio would not only be boring, but annoying. Only my grandparents know that story well; only they can tell it. I've only been around for eighteen years, and other than speaking a little of their career, I can only talk about what I've seen, which isn't much. I don't have any anecdotes; I can't make anyone laugh or cry with my vague memories of their past. I can't even describe any of it because it's been a long time since I've seen them perform before an audience. Yes, I've heard them play at home. I know very well that my grandmother prefers to sit during each rehearsal, always in the chair beside the door. My grandfather and Juan, the second voice, sit on a long sofa right across from her. The rehearsals and shows always follow tracks and sequences, which are necessary because my grandfather plays the guitar and Juan the requinto guitar, but they have no bass or percussion. On a CD player that looks ancient and makes me feel a little nostalgic, my grandmother plays the CD with the tracks. The songs almost always have a countdown, so my grandfather and Juan know when to come in. You hear the countdown and they start playing while my grandmother prepares to surprise us all with her voice, which at every turn is more tired and more alive. She waits her turn; she moves her head to the rhythm of the music that's already begun, and then she comes in. I'd like you to hear the song I'm listening to as I write this. I'd like to describe that melody. I've watched them practise so many times; I've been listening to them my whole life. I know all those songs perfectly, the rhythms, the lyrics. It felt like they intended to incorporate us into their musical legacy without asking if that was what we wanted. They began training us when we were small, and we were almost ready, but I just didn't have that diva smile, while my sister lacked the posture. We lacked artistic charm and stage presence. I lacked the desire.

I've always heard their voices in live performance. My grandmother hasn't heard of lip-synching, and

I doubt she'd be interested. There are melodies I've only heard from them, melodies whose original singers I don't know. Songs I will always remember in my grandmother's voice.

What would another child do in my position? What would a kid think if she'd never heard music like this in a live performance, much less in her own living room?

What would this child do if one day she woke up to the music resounding in her house and, opening the door to the living room, discovered her own grandparents there, her aunt, cousin, mother, sister, everyone singing? Would she be surprised to discover that the family she'd heard singing from the other side of the door...was her own?

I'm the one on the other side of that door. My sister and I are the ones who've always sat through rehearsals at home, who've heard the same songs again and again with all the mistakes you don't hear in performance. We've sung boleros and tangos as if those were our own music. But they're not. That's not our music, though we do enjoy it.

*

I like to sing in my living room.

Several days ago, watching a video from when I was small – I couldn't have been more than three years old – I saw myself dancing in that same living room, with a hairbrush for a microphone. That was me. When I saw myself, I laughed; I looked adorable. I could barely even speak, but I could carry a tune. Mom watched the video too, and she told me that the song I was singing was one she'd been learning that day. She was rehearsing, and I joined her. It has always been a normal thing to watch my family rehearse, and also something I enjoy. I was very happy to see myself in that video. I haven't changed much; even now I sing while pretending to hold a microphone. I still stand in the middle of the living room and imagine that there are thousands of people listening to me, and I listen to them as they scream my name and sing along. I stand at the edge of the stage and lean down and offer high fives; I wave and jump around and dance. And I walk around the living room with its white floor tiles, but I don't step on them. I stay on the little path of black tiles. That's the edge of the stage. I listen and watch all this until the song is over and I have to go to the computer and start another one before the audience screams for more. I love it all. I enjoy it without knowing if this is really my thing or just something I've gotten used to. Is it me, from within, desiring to be the kind of famous singer that so many in my family tried to become? Or was it them who got me used to this, who groomed me to become the star that none of them could ever be?

*

One afternoon, Mom's boss made her leave the house running. He told her he needed her urgently at the restaurant. She got out of bed, got ready in less than five minutes, and then stood before him. She closed the office door, greeted him with a smile, and said, "Hey, thanks for calling me. I just wanted to let you know that this weekend I have a rehearsal for – you know, my show, and –"

Mom's boss interrupted her. He raised his right hand to silence her. Then he spoke.

"Hold on. I think there's no better time than now to make a request. I've been wanting to work something out with you."

"Oh, okay. What is it?" she asked, struck by the distant tone of this man she considered a friend.

"I think it's time for you to start treating me as you should. As an employee treats a manager," he said.

This stopped Mom in her tracks. She swallowed and answered.

"Oh, okay. If that's what you want."

"Listen: I think that little show is taking up too much of your time," he said rudely, contempt clear in his voice.

"I really don't think that affects my work here though. It's a different schedule than the restaurant's," she said nervously. Her voice trembled nervously as the words fell from her mouth.

"Yes, that was true at first. But now you're asking for time off, and you're not rehearsing. I thought you understood that you can't just show up here and sing anything; you have to practise; you have to be committed," he said with a pause, chilly. "I suggest you start managing your time better. That's all."

He gestured toward the door without looking at her.

Mom looked at him in anger; she was sad, confused. She closed the door and turned toward home. She locked herself in her room and stayed there for the whole day. I decided to leave her alone, and I hoped that maybe later she'd tell me what had happened. When she didn't open the door, when she didn't even come out to talk, I knocked on the door and tried to hear her talking to herself, a distant murmur that faded in and out, a sniffly nose and a low, almost silent cry. She didn't open the door or say anything.

*

After that afternoon, Mom kept on working at the restaurant. On one of her many work nights she left looking as gorgeous as always; she wore a red dress that still fits her along with some cream-coloured high heels. She also wore a long necklace that fell between her breasts. She wore her cat-like makeup, dark lipstick and blush. I said goodbye to her as she got into the elevator.

Soon, it was 1 a.m., and Mom wasn't back.

"She said she'd be home by midnight," I said to my little sister, who looked at me with her big blue eyes. She didn't know what to say and kept on playing.

It was late, quite late for Mom to still be out. It was 2 a.m. She still wasn't home. I wanted to go out looking for her, but I couldn't, not at that hour. I was scared.

*

My image of her: she is running, running away. I don't know where she's going. She doesn't like this place; she really doesn't like any place. She only wants to escape.

Of course I have other images of her: she is so much more than anything she's wanted or tried to be. She's more than the things she has done. But that is what I remember now: a mother who wanted to go away, who was never content. A mother who didn't like Medellín. I couldn't understand it. That and other things, but especially that. Why didn't she like it here? Why was she always trying to go elsewhere? And, worse than that, why hadn't she managed to do it?

I know Mom is looking for something more. She's told us so. Sometimes it's almost as if she was trying to convince us that there - whatever *there* might mean - is better than here. I have told her many times that I like the place where I was born.

"If I could, I'd stay here forever, Mom," I tell her.

I don't know if that would convince her. Or if it would convince me. But I need her to know that I'm not going to follow her around for the rest of my life. If she wants to escape, then so do I.

Now there have been many times when she's attempted to escape. Among them, the one I least remember is the one most mentioned in our family: her trip to the USA. According to the story, I was a year and a half. Her career was building. She was a young, beautiful woman with a normal life, not much going on. Already married. From a musical family. Talented. She only had one thing tying her down: a daughter. Her first. Me.

Mom had been waiting for an opportunity like this for some time. She sent out photos, resumes, videos and songs wherever she could, until someone called back. Discos Fuentes was the first record label to sign her. She recorded as much as she could; she was the main voice in several of their songs. She also recorded videos. She was a recognized face in a few groups, but important ones, at least for her. Discos Fuentes was looking for a great artist, and they saw that potential in Mom. A few months after her success in Colombia, they wanted her to travel to the USA for three months with an orchestra they'd put together. She was ready; she had the time; she had lots of ambition and her whole life ahead of her. Oh... There was me. But that didn't matter. Above all else, she had herself. Beautiful, talented, enthusiastic. She packed her things, said goodbye to her mother, waved, cried a little. It wasn't the end of the world. She left. Three months, I think. That's what they always say. I don't know the details; I don't know that side of the story. I know what happened here while she was gone. They've told me about it many times.

My grandparents were the ones who took care of me. I've seen videos from that time, in which they ask me to sing for Mom, to imitate the way she left.

"Okay sweetie, look at the camera."

And once I finally turn around:

"What did Mom do when she left? Come on, show us."

And I just manage to move my hand a little as if saying goodbye.

There's one video I remember: I'm singing in the living room in front of a walled mirror we had, convinced that no one could see me. Like a natural artist, like the innocent child it was, I start singing. Right there, facing the mirror, evaluating each movement. I rate myself, trying to determine if I'm actually made for this. I move around the room, holding the brush that has always been a microphone; I sing the way I've always liked to and still do – alone. My grandmother recorded me without me noticing. I wasn't alone and only know that now, eighteen years later. In any case, right there, in the living room full of mirrors, I am singing. I don't remember if the song ended because my grandmother was tired of recording or because I saw she was watching and ran away from the scene. In any case, I stopped singing, and my grandmother forgot to cut immediately; with the camera facing the floor her broken voice declared, "This will make your Mom cry."

The recording cut. And I ask myself if my Mom cried the way my grandmother imagined she would.

I don't remember anything from those times, but my grandmother says the doctors were sure that this experience would mark me. That the episode of depression I had then at the age of one and a half would repeat itself in my adolescence and adulthood; that it would always stem from my relationship with my mother. I was not well; I had high fevers; I cried constantly; I was not happy. But when I was taken to the doctor, all the tests came back normal. There was nothing wrong with me - at least, nothing physically wrong. Mom found out what was happening and had to come home. We were both too small for this to be happening. I was too small for her to have gone away. And she was too small, too young to stay in one place. To come home.

I think, though it's only a guess, that this experience was at the root of her decision to go off travelling once again, but this time taking us with her. By that point there were three of us: Mom, my sister and me. A few months earlier, Mom had met this man: pallid and pot-bellied, with a blonde moustache as pale as the rest of his face and part of his head. He smiled a lot, at least when he saw my sister and me. At first, Mom introduced him to us as a friend who'd come from far away. That surprised me. He didn't know us, neither my sister nor me, and yet he'd come from far away to visit us. Then came the real surprise: he was actually

Mom's boyfriend. Though she never said it. She never said anything. I had to figure it out, to put two and two together after reading the signs. If I needed answers, I'd have to make them up.

The fact that they were a couple was a bit of a blow. It's because Mom wasn't one to be involved with men, much less in that moment when she only wanted to sing. But, above all else, it was difficult for me to believe that he was her boyfriend. She wasn't one for pale, pot-bellied men. I remember and reaffirm my theory: she did not go for that type at all. Three months later she gave him the last of his roles, the definitive one:

"He's my manager."

I found this off-putting. I didn't really understand Mom's decisions, but this one seemed the most absurd of all. Why did she introduce him in so many different ways if she knew that the last one would be the most pleasing to our family: a simple manager? My grandmother smiled. He was Mom's manager; that meant that she hadn't abandoned her hope of becoming a singer, of making a living from music, of travelling for music. My grandmother rejoiced over this; she asked Mom questions and pressured her for a while, expecting this supposed manager to show results. If anything had managed to take my grandmother's focus off her own singing career, it was her daughter's career. There wasn't much left to hope for from her own, and my aunt, the eldest daughter, had never wanted to follow that path, at least not directly. Therefore there was no other choice; the most important career was

Mom's. Even though that was not a recent decision....
after the tour of the USA, when my grandmother had
stayed here with me, the determination was growing.
No, even before that, when the trio had to come back
from Mexico because my great-grandmother had gotten
sick and couldn't care for the children. The three children
my grandparents had left behind, cared for by my mother's grandmother. Since then. Since that failure, when the
trio came back, and my grandmother seemed set on aban-
doning her life as an artist. That didn't happen, of course.
They don't travel now, but it's as if they've kept on hoping
for some sign, some call. Some opportunity.

My grandmother was clear in her decision to take
care of us while Mom went on tour with an orchestra
organized by her friend/boyfriend/manager, whom I
just thought of as Mr. Pot-Bellied Pale Man. In fact,
she spent a few days trying to convince Mom that the
best thing would be for her to go alone. She'd be here
to take care of us while Mom developed as an artist.
My grandmother clearly wanted to put Mom's career
first. And the thought of Mom going off to work in
another country with two small children – one seven
and the other four – seemed ridiculous and impossible
to my grandmother.

But Mom had made her decision. This time we would
go with her. The destination was El Salvador, that small
Central American nation.

*

Since the trip, the tour, the work and lodging were all under the control of the pot-bellied pale man, Mom could play the diva role and just sit back and let things happen.

The man seemed worried; he talked on the phone all day, pacing around the house; he sent emails and supervised (or pretended to supervise) each of the orchestra's rehearsals. According to Mom, he was doing a lot of work. She, on the other hand, dedicated herself to rehearsing, to trying on sparkly dresses and getting all her papers ready for the day of the trip. She stated many times that the country we were travelling to was better than any other. We only knew our own country and didn't have much to compare it to, but that didn't matter. Whatever Mom said had to be true.

One or two months before leaving, Mom decided to share her plans with us. She told us that her idea was for us to stay there in El Salvador. This scared me. I thought of my grandparents, my friends. For the first time I gave a lot of thought to the place where I lived, and I didn't want to leave it. Not permanently. Mom had never suggested something like this. For me, Colombia was the only place to live; there was no other option and I was not seeking anything else. But in that moment staying put was no longer the only option. In fact, it was no longer an option at all. We'd soon be on our way.

My family was happy. My grandmother was thrilled. I hoped to go and come back quickly, but someone had already packed my things; someone had already made plans for me. Mom had decided for me, and there was nothing I could do.

The months went by and soon we were at the airport. The whole orchestra waited without sleeping until 2 a.m., the time to board the plane. We sat together, conversing and fighting off our drowsiness. I stayed beside Mom, who held my sister in her lap. My sister seemed to be paying attention to what the adults were saying, but there was nothing beyond her childlike gaze that remained fixed on a point straight ahead. With her blue eyes half open and her ecstatic little smile, it looked like she fully understood what they were talking about. I didn't pay too much attention to what I heard, instead focusing on the faces. I could see the tiredness; they had bags under their eyes and yawned frequently, but they were animated by the hope of success. They were eager to travel to an unknown country where maybe things would work out for the best.

I resisted falling asleep, and I remained on guard against something – I don't know what – until they called us to board. Everyone stood up except for my sister who had allowed herself a nap that wouldn't end until we reached El Salvador.

The flight was short; three hours aren't much. The first news our family back home heard of us was of the moment we stepped off the plane. El Salvador had plenty to tell us.

The orchestra's performances had been programmed before we left; for that reason the pale, pot-bellied man looked stressed. He wanted things to come off like a gust of wind, like a video that might be rewound or fast-forwarded according to the viewer's wishes. But life continued its normal course and the weeks passed slowly for him. For me they went very fast.

*

I enjoyed El Salvador very much. I forgot all the fear I'd once had of not returning home. I loved the climate, the food, our apartment; that apartment that was not ours but already held our scent and our things. Also, in order to avoid making the change too hard on us, Mom signed us up for summer school, where we studied math, language and science. Strangely, though, the school placed an emphasis on the arts.

When we got there, we couldn't avoid it: our new classmates were surprised and interested in us, the two Colombian girls. We became popular. This type of attention was always been my preference: I like praise from up close more than the screams of a large audience. It was fun how every morning they'd sit in a circle and want to listen to stories of our lives which they saw as taking place far away in a different country. In that moment we were living a life that wasn't really ours, that didn't really belong to us. We'd invaded their space and their world; they seemed charmed by this. To hear them ask about Colombia, as if it was a truly faraway place, one they only heard about in the news, made us laugh. I felt a certain pity for them. Colombia was beautiful to me but unknown to so many; Colombia, which I knew so well, which was so very much mine, was a mystery to others. Colombia was my secret and the fact that they knew so little about it was an advantage; we could talk as if it were an incredible, fantastic place, and after that we could change perspectives and tell terrible tales, assuring them that everything they saw on TV was true, that we'd arrived in El Salvador fleeing from the many wars they asked us about. Playing with reality was fun. Knowing that they would never – at least not soon – find out that we were lying gave us a certain kind of power.

*

After three months in that school, where the majority of our assignments were artistic ones, my sister and I stood out not only for our nationality, but also our talent. Right after our first month, all our teachers and friends knew that we could sing, that we came from a musical family. That we were there for one sole reason: to sing. That we planned on staying. That we were planning to make a living there. That in Colombia it was nearly impossible to make a living – only later would we find out that the same was true in El Salvador. My friends, who at first believed that I was nothing more than a new girl from another country, now knew more about us than I liked, and they asked me to sing whenever they were bored.

"Psst...Hey! *Colombiana!*"

"What? What's going on?"

"Sing. Come on. Won't you?"

"Sorry, no. Maybe later."

"Please? Just one song."

Just one song? That was already too much. And that was all. If they asked me for more than one, I'd be spent. A complete song is like an extremely long race, with all the exhaustion, the running out of breath, the need to stay hydrated. The fact that my friends knew I could sing stripped the fun from our false stories about Colombia and the whole fictitious life my sister and I had invented for ourselves. We couldn't lie anymore. And worse, we couldn't hide our talent, which is what we'd wanted to do from the start. Now the only thing I could do was refuse to sing, and that's what I did. My talent – that talent that I'm not even sure is mine, that might as easily be imposed on me as real – was kept secret for a few weeks. During that time I was selfishly silent. And happy.

One day my mother received a letter from the school – a letter that I myself handed to her, following my teacher's orders.

"I need you to give this note to your mother," she said, smiling, with her eyes wide open, as if she thought this bright expression would help me understand more fully what she was asking me to do.

"Okay," I said, shrugging my shoulders quickly.

"Promise me you will," she said, widening her eyes even more.

"I promise."

I walked toward the car where Mom and the pot-bellied man were waiting. They were both smiling; they had good news for us, while I was holding in my hands a trivial note from school. We made it home and they told us to stay in the living room. The living room was my favourite place. It was spacious and – just like the one in Bogotá, where I'd sit years later – it let the sun and wind in. The Salvadoran wind fulfilled the same need that the musicals would later fulfill in Bogotá: it saved us from boredom and loneliness. The wind that came in violently over the balcony helped us keep our imagination moving and turned out to be our favourite toy. Stepping out onto the balcony, closing the door and waiting for the wind was the boring part, but when it came it shook up everything. My sister and I stood in the middle of the balcony, where there was only one Rimax chair, nothing more, and at any hour the wind would come to startle us, to trick us with its fake sweetness. We stayed like that, my sister and I, receiving the gentle wind, inventing a dialogue between two friends who ask each other why the wind is blowing today if in El Salvador it's always calm. We had to act too because the wind demanded a good performance. The two friends began to feel that the wind was getting stronger, and that scared them, so they decided to call the emergency number with the excuse that the wind never blew and today it seemed like all the palm trees were about to fall over. But the call didn't go through, or the signal was damaged, and the wind blew even more furiously. It dragged us along the balcony; the friends in our little play were dragged along the city's main street. It messed up our hair, made our hearts beat faster. It was ruthless; it seemed angry and made us fall; it lifted us off the ground a little, and we had to grab onto the door. Afraid, charmed, laughing, Mom watched us from the living room. She only managed to hear the wind – along with our bodies – hitting the glass windows that led to the balcony; she'd have to imagine or remember our laughter. We listened to the hum of the wind in our ears; we looked twenty floors down where life went on as always; then we turned, watching each other make faces, laughing like mimes, letting ourselves be moved abruptly by the wind and, when we noted that we could not hear anything more than the wind, our laughter returned, the emptiness in our stomachs, and we fell down on the balcony floor, on the edge of erupting in laughter. That must have been our favourite game. We played it as many times as we liked and never got bored. We'd return, rent that imagined apartment again and embrace the strong, gentle wind again. We played until the day when it blew so fiercely that tears fell from our eyes; it stripped my sister of her clothing and hurled the Rimax chair twenty floors to the ground. Mom intervened and said game over. Enough was enough.

But that afternoon we were there in the living room, not playing, not laughing, waiting for who knows what. Mom said she had good news; the pot-bellied man smiled and hugged us, waiting for our reaction. I looked on suspiciously. Without a word, Mom gestured for us to wait and then dug into her purse without looking until she found what she wanted and impulsively pulled out the long-awaited object.

"Tada!" she said in a melodic voice.

It wasn't immediately clear what the big surprise was; I just saw two pieces of paper in her hands. Suddenly, I felt the heavy hand of the pot-bellied man on my shoulder; he turned me around and asked me what I thought. I smiled and, simultaneously nervous and delighted, said, "I don't know what that is."

They both erupted in loud laughter, as if expecting this response, and Mom said, "They're tickets, my love. You're both invited to hear the orchestra tonight. What do you think?"

This was to be our first time attending one of Mom's concerts, so of course I was excited. I was happy; I thanked them and spent the whole afternoon asking when we would go, if we truly were going, if she'd already asked if we children would be allowed in. Since all the questions had been answered more than three times, I decided to pack a little purse to make sure it would be my best night ever. I grabbed a little mirror Mom had given me, a chocolate the pot-bellied man had given me that morning, and a daily planner where I wrote down anything I considered important. I felt that something was missing, and I sat down on the bed to think long and hard about things I didn't even have, things that nevertheless would be amazing that night. And after so much thinking and staring at the same spot in my bag, I remembered the note from school that I'd brought home for Mom.

Mom was a little stressed about the show, but for me that was as good a moment as any to speak, to ask questions, to get in her way. I approached Mom, who was putting on her makeup; I grabbed the sleeve of her dress and timidly asked, "Mom?"

She turned around, trying to hide the effort it took for her to look away from the mirror. With her eyes only, she asked me to leave her alone. She smiled and I thought that meant I could speak, but once again she turned back to the mirror. Daringly, I spoke again: "Mom, today the school sent a note home."

"I can't read it right now," she said shortly.

"My teacher made me promise to give it to you," I replied.

"But I can't right now, dear. Be patient. I'll read it later."

Then, as now, I wanted everything to take place as quickly as possible. The difference is that then, I tried to insist on making things happen in the moment I desired.

"Mom, I think this is a good time. The teacher seemed really eager to have you read this."

"Don't be demanding. I said no. We're about to go and you're giving me a note that should be read slowly and carefully. Please be patient," she said, now clearly upset.

"I could read it out loud to you."

"Don't make me lose my patience."

I'd pushed Mom to the limit and still wouldn't let up; I clutched the note firmly and, carefully, I opened it. I read, "Dear Ms. Solano, the purpose of this letter is to inform you of an unfortunate incident that occurred yesterday, when your older daughter demonstrated a real lack of interest in the school's..." Silence. I stopped reading. An unfortunate incident? Involving me? A lack of interest? I couldn't remember. It seemed I'd made Mom's blood boil. I walked backwards, thinking I'd manage to leave, let Mom finish her makeup, stand up, call us to get in the truck and go to the concert. But Mom had heard my words.

"Give me that," she said dryly, snatching the note from my hands. "...A real lack of interest in the school's artistic activities. It all started when I asked her to prepare a song for an assembly that we are holding in a few weeks, and she refused. Also, she has said quite rudely that she is tired of singing and that this school does not give her any motivation to continue. She asks for our understanding; she asks us not to expect much from her, particularly because this assembly is not something that interests her. She says that she refuses to participate in these types of activities, both now and in the future. Ms. Solano, we greatly lament the way your daughter's attitude inhibits her talent. This note is simply a request that you do what you can at home to work on her attitude."

Mom dropped the note and, without even looking at me, spoke through gritted teeth, "All right. Not tonight, I guess."

"What?" I asked nervously, sadly. I knew what she was talking about.

She turned around, looked at me and said, "Not tonight. No concert for you. If you refuse to make music, if you find it so distasteful that you don't even want to do it, there's no reason for you to go to a concert."

So that night there was no show, not for me. Mom was not harsh or strict, but that note showed her something inside me she hadn't been aware of, something she did not share and probably had never experienced: an apathy toward music. But I didn't want to stop singing. At that time I was just starting to learn new techniques to sing better. My possible talent was something I merely suspected I had, but that journey, those concerts, seeing Mom go out each night to sing made me think that there was no reason to sing out of a sense of obligation. Why not just do it for fun? And that was why I didn't want to sing at school – I wanted to do it for myself, to see what would happen if I just sang for my own enjoyment. Of course it didn't lead to anything good. Mom punished me for not wanting to make music, and I was not allowed to hear the orchestra until the following month, in a hotel restaurant, at 7 p.m., in what would be, without me knowing or even suspecting it, the group's last concert in El Salvador.

*

When we'd barely started on the road to where the
orchestra would play that night, everyone was absorbed in
conversation, including my sister and me. We were always
really shy around Mom's musicians, so we'd comment on
this or that just to hide how nervous and giddy we were.
The dancers were talking and flirtatiously laughing; the
musicians were shouting, making noise, practically hanging
out the windows, and it became clear that our drivers were
not in a good mood, already tired of the job. The venue was
one hour outside the city centre where we lived, and we
couldn't tell if time was flying or if the journey was very long;
we didn't know if this strange passage of time was working
for us or against us, but eventually we got there. We arrived
and the place was very large; at least, that was how it looked

from the outside. We were all waiting on the bus, anxious. Everyone was moving and making their own gestures, as if secretly praying or talking to themselves. That moment of waiting seemed like a ritual that had already taken place. All were waiting in silence; we heard nothing but a few people's muffled prayers. With trembling hands the dancers touched up their makeup; the musicians paced around the bus, sometimes bumping into one another, but nothing interrupted their mantras. It was as if they were about to perform for the first time in their lives. My sister and I remained silent, respecting this established ritual, and also because we didn't know what our role in this moment was supposed to be. We focused on watching them walk, tremble and laugh at themselves when they realized how nervous they were. It was strange seeing them like this because it wasn't what I had imagined. At rehearsal they all seemed confident, on top of their game. Now they all looked like bundles of nerves.

Before getting off the bus, Mom gathered everyone, asking them to give thanks, to send good energy and, almost as a last resort, to ask God for all to go well. And so, after that little prayer, some hugs, and good energy passed around, the orchestra members got off the bus. My sister and I followed the pot-bellied man who attended all the performances to observe, dance and drink. This time he was also supposed to be taking care of us.

When we entered, we were surprised by the place. It was a restaurant in an enormous hotel. I thought El Salvador was too small for such extravagance. What I actually thought to myself was, "It's amazing that this big a restaurant even fits inside such a small country." I didn't go into the hotel; I didn't have time. All night long I remained watching the orchestra and checking out each corner of the restaurant, which was typically Central American. Cowboy hats were offered to all who entered; there were cactus decorations, snakes hanging everywhere, colourful borders on the walls, flags of El Salvador and a Virgin Mary icon set before the stage. Everything was vibrant and colourful. There were three hundred folding chairs on the first level and nearly one hundred on the second. The stage was about a metre high, with lights all around it; from the second level my sister and I could see much better, so we chose to sit up there for the show we'd waited so long to see. We sat at the table that was right at the edge of the balcony; we could lean over the railing. The pot-bellied man smiled at us the whole time, as if he approved of our decisions. He let us sit where we wanted and order whatever we liked. We ordered some nachos and waited for the concert to begin. Half an hour later, the orchestra members took their places. No one announced them; they entered in silence, and each one took up his or her instrument; they glanced at the percussionist, who counted the beats to begin. The few people seated in that large room were immediately excited. The song began, and Mom entered followed by two dancers. She was already singing, and once they reached centre stage, the dancers began their routine. Mom moved separately from them, with her own steps, prioritizing her voice. I sat there, captivated; nothing could take my gaze from that stage. Mom looked gorgeous, standing there at centre stage, singing as if no one could see her, with her short, brilliant dress, her makeup, her voice. After about a half an hour, the place was full. I then understood why there was so much space and so much decoration: the owners knew that people would come. It didn't look like a hotel restaurant; it was more like a club or private party. People from all over the city were there, even though the restaurant was not centrally located, not near anyone's home, but it had its reputation...or else, maybe the orchestra members had called all these people. People danced; Mom knew how to make them get up and move. She has always looked beautiful dancing onstage. Her dresses are lovely, her charisma, her dances: to sing and follow choreography at once is in my view very admirable. But there is something about her that I can't explain: her talent. The people enjoyed a lot that night: dresses, choreography, pretty faces and music made for dancing, but perhaps no one realized her true talent as she hit those high and low notes. It was the talent of a voice that strives to interpret a piece – an interpretation that goes beyond just getting the notes right. Maybe that night required more than just a good atmosphere or an audience that could enjoy the event. It needed someone to take note of her talent. I hoped my mother could see me there in the audience, enthralled by her voice alone.

It was so late that I expected the sun to come out soon. The orchestra finished after encores. The musicians were tired and a little drunk, but everything seemed fine. The dancers got on the bus quickly and changed out of their high heels as if begging for mercy – they'd had to dance through various songs without choreography, and I watched them make their best efforts to improvise – the musicians first packed their instruments into cases and then quickly got on the bus and collapsed into their seats. My sister and I were already in the bus as they were coming in; she'd fallen asleep earlier, and I'd fallen asleep and woken up several times. We were all ready to go home; we were all in need of rest. But Mom wasn't there. We waited about fifteen minutes, and she didn't show up. I was worried. I asked them to let me get out, but they wouldn't get out of my way. I said Mom might need me, and they laughed. "Please, let me get out," I said. No one answered.

"And what are you going to do, little girl? You're better off waiting here."

And they laughed. Meanwhile, I thought, "Let me do what I'm supposed to; let me save my Mom like I've always done, or at least like I've always tried to do."

Mom appeared. She looked a little upset. She got in and told the driver to get going. He was in no hurry to follow her orders. She was standing close to him, nervous. She trembled. Suddenly, she made a brisk gesture and turned around to see him, the manager, the pale, pot-bellied man, her boyfriend or friend, running toward the bus. He looked angry; he shouted that we'd better not leave him. Mom ordered the driver to get going, please; she moved her hands quickly and, close to him, told him to hurry – more than one swear word slipped out of her mouth. I'd never seen her look so scared; everyone in the bus was watching us without knowing what was happening. The driver decided to get going. I watched the white pot-bellied man running behind the bus until his lungs couldn't stand it anymore and he had to rest with his hands on his knees.

We got home and Mom told us to start packing. My sister was crying due to the exhaustion, the rough way Mom woke her up, the fear. Mom was crying too, but I didn't know why. I watched the whole scene, perplexed.

We packed and left the house; Mom stopped at the side of the road and held out her right hand. A taxi stopped.

One hour later, we were at the airport, waiting for a flight we hadn't planned on, our suitcases filled. We slapped our own foreheads when we remembered things we'd left on tables in our bedrooms, in the living room, alongside the television, on the balcony. Mom seemed calmer, stroking my sister's head which lay in her lap. I got up and leaned my face against the glass that separated the waiting area from the landing strip. I watched the planes arriving and leaving; I watched the sun coming out. I turned and saw Mom; I saw my suitcase. I thought about Colombia, the orchestra, all the musicians, the dancers who weren't with us now. They called us to board the flight, and at last I wept.

*

Mom was delayed, but she did come back from work that night in Bogotá. They fired her. She stayed late crying in the restaurant. Have I told you she's dramatic? Well, this time I'll give her the benefit of the doubt. I can imagine that her conversation with the restaurant owner was quite intense. Let's suppose he mentioned everything she'd done wrong. Maybe he said she lacked discipline and the other workers were saying bad things about her. "It's clear she doesn't practise." "She always gets in late." "She doesn't pay her bill." "She's boring the customers." Poor Mom. Her work depended - and still depends - on an ability to entertain the customers. If the diners lose interest in her, the other workers experience it as their own failing. So let's suppose they spoke badly of her. All this hurt, but it didn't break her. She had one easy answer to all those comments, but the owner had more arguments:

"Also, your level of performance has gone way down. What happened to that singer I met in Medellín?" Surely here he lowered his gaze, thought for a moment, and said, "I'm disappointed to realize your talent is not what I thought. Don't misunderstand me - I am disappointed in myself, for my choice. I've always been good at knowing who has real talent and who does not."

Poor Mom. Those words broke her, if that's the sort of thing he said. Let's imagine it was. Let's imagine that she stayed there all night, sitting at the bar, maybe on the corner, talking to the cook who'd been such a good friend to us. Talking about nothing. Asking him things he didn't know about or didn't want to discuss. She cried until he told her that she'd be better off getting some rest.

"There's nothing more you can do. Go home and sleep. Your girls are probably waiting up for you."

I was awake. I waited up until she came home. She opened the door carefully. I rushed to meet her, relieved to see her alive, angry that she was alive. She was so late, and I was terrified.

"Mom -" I said.

"We have to go back to Medellín, my love," she said softly, her voice filled with sadness.

She gave me a big hug and went to bed. I wanted an explanation. So did she.

*

It doesn't hurt to go back.

Our apartment in Medellín is small. Right in the entryway there's a dining room connected to the living room - a TV and an old rocking chair - with three bedrooms in the back: one for Mom, one for my sister, and one for me. The kitchen is in the front, separated from the entryway by a little wall; it's small and leads to the laundry room. When we came home, everything was as we had left it. Nothing had changed. The weather was the same; the apartment was the same, just a little dusty. At school our friends and teachers had nothing new to report. To me it seemed incredible that our life had taken so many twists and turns in such a short time, while here, nothing had changed. It seemed incredible and also a little unnecessary. We could have just stayed, living here in our familiar environment with the people we knew. In the end we were just going to come back anyway. But I think Mom had to go through this, to try again for her dream. And she needed to take us with her so as not to come back to an empty house each day.

When we went to El Salvador I was seven years old. In Bogotá I was thirteen. In Medellín I've been nearly all the other ages. Right now, for example, I'm eighteen.

I've been in many of Mom's music classes; I've observed them; I've been her student. I've been at rehearsals, concerts. I've met many musicians. It was normal to see them here at home some mornings drinking coffee. I recorded choir performances for Mom, radio jingles, full songs. I was the main singer in her youth choir for a long time before she decided to stop leading it. I wrote lyrics, melodies. Not that long ago I tried to form my own group; I couldn't; I didn't want to. I've tried to adapt. I haven't been able to, but things haven't changed because of this. I keep recording songs whenever she wants; a few days ago I got up at night because she needed my voice in some chorus parts. I continue to listen to conversations among musicians whom most people would see as unreachable stars.... but I know them as normal working people who just want a cup of coffee in anyone's home. I keep watching rehearsals, accompanying her to concerts, following her. Every so often I hear her talking to someone about how talented I am; every so often she tells me how talented I am.

Mom keeps on going out with her lovely dresses; she keeps on singing; she keeps on; she keeps on. I also sing, of course, nearly all day long. The difference is that I do it just for myself. Not that long ago I met a writer. He told me that for twenty years he threw everything he wrote into the fireplace; he'd get an idea, sit down, grab his paper and pencil, and slowly draw out each scene, describing characters, moments, feeling, everything with the naturalness of a spring flowing from his head down to his hands. He put all his feeling onto the page, but then looked at it in surprise; he reread it, smiling, satisfied; he nodded and turned his chair around. He got up, reached the fireplace, bent down to feel the heat in his face, and then fearlessly threw what he'd just written into the fire. He knew he was talented; he knew he could easily do something better than this the next day; but, above all else, he knew that he wanted his talent to be his alone, an intimate part of him. For twenty years he burned his writings. How much we'd have if he hadn't done that! But then, who would he be? Publishing at such a young age might have overwhelmed him; for a while, he wanted to keep it all to himself. There was no audience, no spectacle. Readers will only remember what's been published; the rest is lost, forgotten.

Singing is an act that belongs to the past. Speaking also. What I say is in the past; even I don't remember it. My words are forgotten, my thoughts, my songs. What I sang yesterday no longer exists. The difference is that among the audience, the witnesses, there are those who make it hard to forget. If one person hears what you have to say, they might remember it; if there are two, it becomes much more probable. This is the explanation: people seek fame because they fear being forgotten. But I don't.

Mom wants to be famous. That is why she has sung everywhere, recording a thousand songs; that is why she can be heard each day on the radio.

Mom, you've tried so many times. You've tried to run away; you've tried to stay. You've been forced to accept what you have, and later you reject it. You've tried, above all, to make your living doing this, but you know it's not easy. You've tried to convince me of my talent, to persuade me that a musical career is for me. We've had conversations in which you tell me everything you expect of me and then, when we finish and there are no arguments left on either side, you sit on the edge of your bed and lament, trying to accept that your inheritance stops with you. You couldn't pass music on to me. I didn't want it.

You've tried to accept that I want something else, even though you know I can't get away from all this so easily. You've watched me writing; you walk down the hall and see my door ajar. You can't go by there without wanting to open the door and see the pathetic sight: a young 18-year-old girl trying to write, putting words together. Some sound good; others sound ridiculously awful. I feel your presence in the room and lift my eyes to see you watching me with a little smile that feigns pride. You open your eyes a little wider and ask, "How's the book coming along?"

You're not convinced that it's a book, and really, neither am I. I don't know what it will be, nor do you know what it's about, though you know you're the only thing I have to write about, to talk about. I answer that it's going fine, that I'm nervous, that I want to get it done, that it's been painful to write, or else I just think that and say, in a dry, faltering voice, "Fine."

You smile and nod, then step back and close the door. I don't know what you expect, nor what I do. Maybe my hope is that you will accept this; that your smile is a sincere one as you watch me sitting down trying to write something, that you will accept my choice and not insist that I follow your path. But you, perhaps, hope that I will give up, that we'll both sit down and laugh at the memory of how once I tried to change this fate that happened to be ours.

I can't be sure I've chosen something else, nor can I say that I've truly given up on music. This voice is the only thing I have. It will follow me wherever I go.

*